The Man with the Violin

The Man with the Violin

Kathy Stinson · Dušan Petričić

annick press
toronto + berkeley + vancouver

© 2013 Kathy Stinson (text)
© 2013 Dušan Petričić (illustrations)
© 2013 Joshua Bell (postscript)
Designed by Dušan Petričić and Sheryl Shapiro
First paperback printing, March 2016
Credits: photo of Joshua Bell on page 33 © Lisa-Marie Mazzucco

Annick Press Ltd.

We acknowledge the support of the Canada Council for the Arts, the Ontario Arts Council, and the participation of the Government of Canada/la participation du gouvernement du Canada for our publishing activities.

Cataloging in Publication

Stinson, Kathy
    The man with the violin / Kathy Stinson ; illustrated by Dušan Petričić.

Issued also in electronic formats.
ISBN 978-1-55451-565-3 (bound) ISBN 978-1-55451-564-6 (pbk)

    I. Petričić, Dušan II. Title.

PS8587.T56M35 2013   jC813'.54   C2013-901235-4

Published in the U.S.A. by Annick Press (U.S.) Ltd.
Distributed in Canada by University of Toronto Press.
Distributed in the U.S.A. by Publishers Group West.

Printed in China

Visit us at: www.annickpress.com
Visit Kathy Stinson at: www.kathystinson.com
Visit Joshua Bell at: www.joshuabell.com

Also available in e-book format. Please visit www.annickpress.com/ebooks for more details. Or scan

To all my musical grandchildren and especially Peter, who even more than the others helps us pay attention to what we might otherwise miss.
—K.S.

For Lara and Rastko.
—D.P.

Dylan was someone who noticed things.

His mom was someone who didn't.

One Friday in January was a day like any other until …

Music!

The high notes soar to the ceiling.
The low notes swoop to the floor.
All the notes swirl and sweep around
the blur of people rushing here and
rushing there. The music is telling
an exciting story. It makes the hairs
on the back of Dylan's neck tickle.

"Mom, wait!"

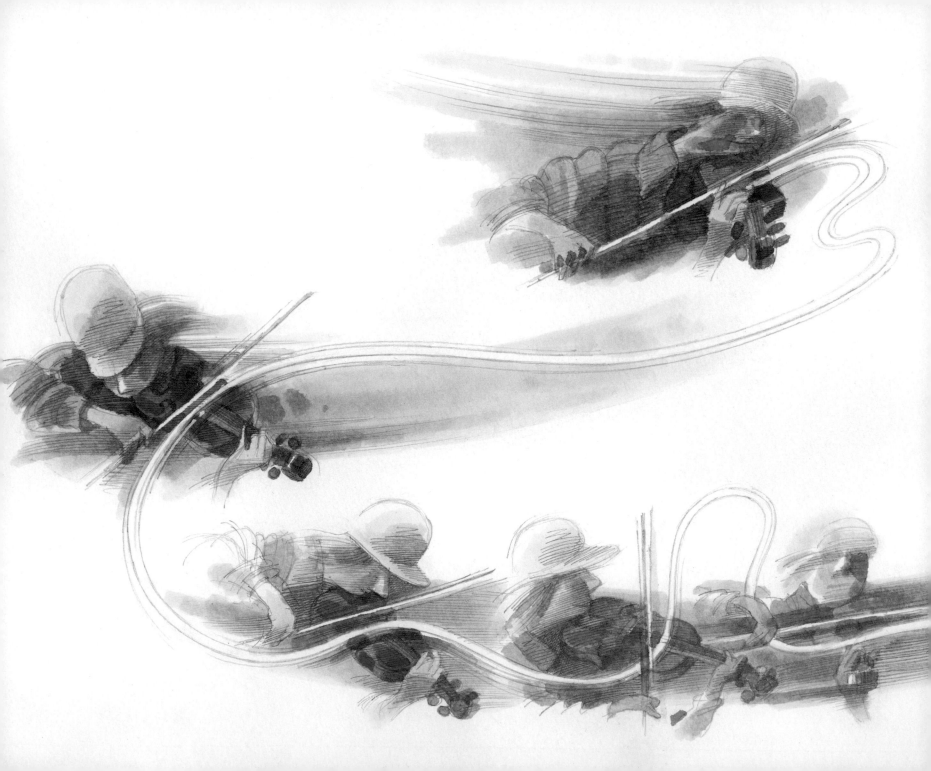

The man with the violin sways this way and that. His fingers move quickly. His bow dances across the strings. The skittering notes make Dylan want to dance too.

Then the music slows and the man's eyes close as if the music is carrying him from *bustle–bustle–bustle* to somewhere far, far away.

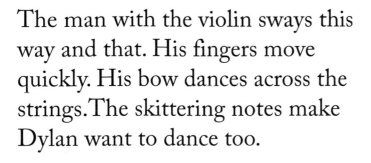

"Please, Mom? Can't we stop? Please?"
If only they could listen for even a minute!

"Not today."

The man with the violin leans forward. His music
makes Dylan's skin hu-u-mmm. Someone begins
shouting, "Blibbity blabbity! Blah blah blah!"
Dylan leans toward the musician, trying to hear.

From the violin comes
the saddest sound he
has ever heard.

The man turns
in his direction.
Their eyes lock.
But the escalator
pulls Dylan
down, down,
down, down,
and away.

Bursting out of the tunnel,
a loud clattering. Dylan strains
to hear the music, but—*grr-rumble
ru-u-umble*—the train gobbles up
the faint notes with its *ro-o-oar*!

All day the music Dylan heard
that morning plays in his head.

On the way home he says,
"Mom, do you think maybe
that man will still be there?"
His mom says, "What man?"

Rain patters.
Dishes clatter.
A voice on the radio
drones on and on
until suddenly …

Music!
Telling a story that makes the apartment
bigger and brighter, and Dylan shouts,
"That's the man in the station!"

The music fades. The voice on the radio says, "Today over a thousand people had the chance to hear one of the finest musicians in the world. Joshua Bell was playing some of the most elegant music ever written, on one of the most valuable violins ever made. Yet few people listened for even a minute."

Dylan says, "I knew it! We should have stopped. We should have listened."

Into a pot of bubbling water spills the spaghetti.

Again the musical story slips and slides
through the air and Dylan can almost
see the man with the violin standing
on tiptoes to reach the high notes.

"Dylan, you're right." His mom turns up the radio. Loud and sweet, the music fills every corner of the apartment.

And together Dylan and his mom dance. Together they listen.

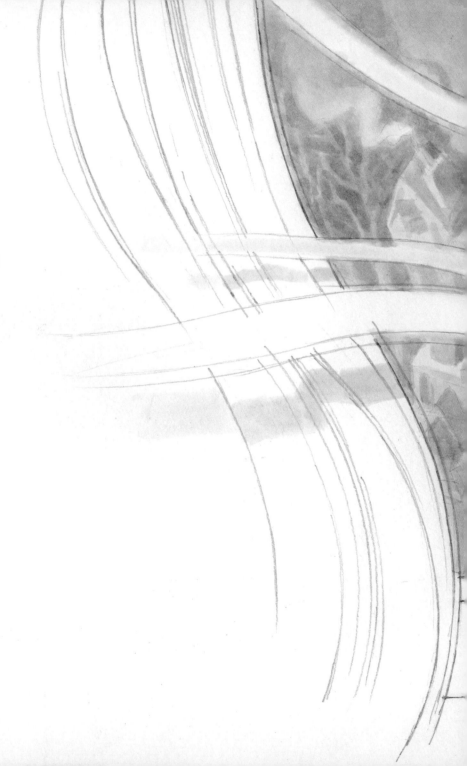

So, is Joshua Bell a real person?

Yes. He was born December 9, 1967, in Bloomington, Indiana. When he was four years old, he tried to make music like he heard on his parents' records by plucking rubber bands that he strung across the handles of dresser drawers. His parents signed him up for violin lessons right away. An early song he taught himself to play was the *Sesame Street* theme song.

By the time he was seven, he played so well he got to perform with the Bloomington Symphony Orchestra and was taking lessons at Indiana University. At 12, he was very serious about his music but he loved playing tennis and computer games too.

Many musicians dream all their lives of playing at Carnegie Hall. Joshua Bell first played there when he was just 17. Then he went to Europe to give concerts in cities where people had already heard what a great violinist he was.

Since then he has given concerts all over the world. He has made over 40 CDs and has often appeared on television. His favorite TV appearance was on *Sesame Street*, when he got to play "Sing After Me" with Telly Monster on tuba.

Someone once said Joshua plays violin "like a god."

Did Joshua Bell really do a concert in a metro station where almost everyone just ignored him?

Yes again. On January 12, 2007, when Joshua Bell took his priceless Stradivarius to L'Enfant Plaza Station in Washington, D.C., he was taking part in an experiment. Someone at a Washington newspaper wanted to see what would happen if one of the best violinists in the world performed there dressed like an ordinary street musician.

He played for 43 minutes. Over 1,000 people walked past. Only seven stopped to listen for more than a minute. No one clapped when he finished a piece. Not after one of the hardest pieces of music ever written. Not even after "Ave Maria," a well-known song that has been making people cry for almost 200 years.

People all over the world pay $100 and more to hear Joshua Bell play in a concert hall. At the end of his concert in the metro station, in the violin case at his feet was $32.17.

There were people passing through the station who wanted to stop but couldn't. Every time a child passed Joshua Bell, he or she tried to stop. But an adult rushed the child along—every time— to wherever they were going.

The boy in *The Man with the Violin* isn't a real boy, but the story tells, and shows, how it might have been for one of the real children who heard Joshua Bell play in the metro station that morning.

Postscript

In January of 2007, over a thousand people *heard* me play my violin in the L'Enfant Plaza Metro Station in Washington, D.C. But very few actually *listened*. Among those who tried were several children, and I clearly remember them turning their heads, straining to listen while their parents dragged them away, hurrying to get to their destination.

Music requires imagination and curiosity—two things that children have aplenty—and I believe the world would be a better place if *every* child's innate appreciation for music were fostered both in school and at home.

My own parents always believed that music was every bit as important in life as mathematics and language, and I will be forever grateful to them for giving me the gift of music in the form of a violin when I was four years old.

Plato is often credited as saying "Music gives soul to the universe, wings to the mind, flight to the imagination, and life to everything."

I couldn't agree more.

Joshua Bell
March, 2013

To download "Ave Maria" and "Estrellita," two of the songs Joshua Bell performed in the subway, go to www.itunes.com/voiceoftheviolin (North America only).

Visit JoshuaBell.com for more information on Joshua Bell and his music.